Goddess Girls

PERSEPHONE
THE PHONY

READ THE OTHER BOOKS IN THE

GODDESS GIRLS SERIES

Athena the Brain

Goddess Girls

PERSEPHONE THE PHONY

JOAN HOLUB & SUZANNE WILLIAMS

NEW YORK   TO   SYDNEY

This book is a work of fiction. Any references to historical events,
real people, or real locales are used fictitiously. Other names, characters,
places, and incidents are the product of the authors' imagination,
and any resemblance to actual events or locales or persons,
living or dead, is entirely coincidental.

ALADDIN

An imprint of Simon & Schuster Children's Publishing Division

1230 Avenue of the Americas, New York, NY 10020

First Aladdin paperback edition April 2010

Copyright © 2010 by Joan Holub and Suzanne Williams

All rights reserved, including the right of reproduction
in whole or in part in any form.

ALADDIN is a trademark of Simon & Schuster, Inc., and related logo
is a registered trademark of Simon & Schuster, Inc.

For information about special discounts for bulk purchases,
please contact Simon & Schuster Special Sales at 1-866-506-1949
or business@simonandschuster.com.

The Simon & Schuster Speakers Bureau can bring authors to your live event.
For more information or to book an event contact the Simon & Schuster Speakers
Bureau at 1-866-248-3049 or visit our website at www.simonspeakers.com.

Designed by Karin Paprocki

The text of this book was set in Baskerville Handcut Regular.

Manufactured in the United States of America

0414 OFF

10

Library of Congress Control Number 2009019176

ISBN 978-1-4169-8272-2

ISBN 978-1-4169-9913-3 (eBook)

CONTENTS

1 THE IMMORTAL MARKETPLACE *Page 1*

2 HADES *Page 16*

3 THE MISSING SANDALS *Page 32*

4 THE SEARCH *Page 40*

5 THE SECOND SANDAL *Page 48*

6 POMEGRANATE SEEDS *Page 59*

7 IN THE UNDERWORLD *Page 72*

8 HOME AGAIN *Page 94*

9 PRINCIPAL ZEUS'S OFFICE *Page 109*

10 THE DANCE *Page 122*

1

The Immortal Marketplace

A LYREBELL PINGED, SIGNALING THE END OF another Monday at Mount Olympus Academy. Persephone crammed the textscroll she'd been reading into her scrollbag and got up to leave the library. As she joined the throng of godboys and goddessgirls streaming into the hallway, a herald appeared on the balcony above them. "The twenty-third day of the school year is now at an end," he announced in a loud, important voice. Then he struck his lyrebell again with a little hammer.

A brown-haired goddessgirl carrying so many scrolls she could barely see over the top of them fell into step beside Persephone. "Ye gods. That means one hundred seventeen days to go!"

"Hi, Athena." Persephone pointed to the pile of scrolls. "Some light reading?" she joked.

"Research," said Athena. She was the brainiest of Persephone's friends, and also the youngest, though they were all in the same grade.

The two goddessgirls continued past a golden fountain. Persephone's eyes flickered over a painting on the wall beyond it, showing Helios, the sun god, mounting to the sky in his horse-drawn carriage. The academy was filled with paintings celebrating the exploits of the gods and goddesses. They were so inspiring!

"Hey, you guys, wait up!" called a goddessgirl in a pale blue chiton—the flowing gown that was all the rage among goddesses and mortal Greek women right now. Aphrodite, the most *gorgeous* of Persephone's friends, raced toward the two girls across gleaming marble tiles. Her long golden hair, held in place by seashell clips, streamed behind her as she dodged past a godboy who was part goat. He bleated, but when he saw who it was, he stared after her with an admiring, doe-eyed look.

"I'm going to the Immortal Marketplace this afternoon," Aphrodite said breathlessly. "Artemis was supposed to go with me, but she's got archery practice. Want to come?"

Athena sagged under her load of scrolls. "I don't

know," she said. "I've got so much work to do."

"It can wait," said Aphrodite. "Don't you want to go shopping?"

"Well," said Athena, "I *could* use some new knitting supplies." Athena was always knitting something. Her last project was a striped woolen cap. She'd made it for Mr. Cyclops, the Hero-ology teacher, to cover his bald head.

"You'll come too, right, Persephone?" Aphrodite asked.

Persephone hesitated. She didn't really want to go to the mall, but she was afraid of hurting Aphrodite's feelings. Too bad she didn't have a good excuse like Artemis. But except for cheering with the Goddess Squad, Persephone wasn't much into sports. "I . . . uh . . . I'd *love* to go," she said at last. Her mom would have been proud. She was always telling Persephone to be polite and "go along to get along."

"Let's stop by my room first," said Aphrodite. "I need to change." Aphrodite was obsessed with clothes and had a different outfit for almost every activity, often changing five or six times a day.

The student dorms were upstairs: girls on the fourth floor and boys on the fifth. Taking the steps two at a time, the goddessgirls were soon at the entrance to the fourth floor. "I'll drop these scrolls in my room and be right there," said Athena.

Aphrodite and Persephone continued down the hall nine more doors. After flinging her bag onto Aphrodite's bed, Persephone perched on the edge of it. "I'll just be a minute," Aphrodite said as she opened her closet.

Persephone glanced around the room. It was small,

but intended for two, with an identical bed, desk, and closet on each side. Aphrodite and Artemis were supposed to have been roommates, but Aphrodite had objected to sharing space with Artemis's three smelly dogs, so Artemis had moved into the room next door. Persephone would've loved to live in the dorm, but her mom insisted that she live at home instead.

Within minutes Aphrodite had wriggled into a fresh chiton—a lavender one this time—and Athena had returned. Back at the entrance to the hall again, the three goddessgirls shucked off their shoes and grabbed winged sandals from a communal basket.

As soon as they slipped them on, the sandals' straps twined around their ankles, and silver wings at their heels began to flap. In a blur of speed, they raced down the marble staircase to the main floor of the academy.

Then, with their feet barely touching the ground, they zipped out the heavy bronze doors and sped across the courtyard. The wind whistled in their ears as they whipped past boulders and trees while descending Mount Olympus.

The Immortal Marketplace stood halfway between the heavens and Earth, below the cloud line. The goddessgirls reached it in minutes, skidding to a stop at the entrance. Loosening the straps around their ankles, they looped them around the silver wings to hold them in place so they could walk at a normal speed.

The marketplace was enormous, with a high-ceilinged crystal roof. Rows and rows of columns separated the various shops selling everything from the newest Greek fashions to tridents and thunderbolts.

Persephone followed Aphrodite and Athena into a shop that sold makeup.

There weren't any clerks, so Aphrodite went directly to one of the counters. A sculpted bust of a beautiful goddess sat on its glass top, surrounded by bottles and boxes of eye powders and liner, creams, and blushes. "Could you make us look like Egyptian princesses?" she asked the statue.

"It would be my pleasure to do so. Please be seated," the statue replied in a polite voice.

Aphrodite perched gracefully on one of the stools and motioned to her two friends to do the same. "Come on, it'll be fun. Just tell the makeup lady what you want." She turned toward the statue. "Egyptian kohl eyes are the newest style."

Almost immediately, three of the boxes opened and brushes flew out, ready to begin powdering the girls' faces.

"No, thanks," said Athena, backing away. "I don't wear makeup."

Her makeup brush paused, almost as if in shock.

"She's young," Aphrodite explained to the brush, trying to soothe it. "Give her a couple of years."

"Ha!" snorted Athena. "You're only ten months older than me. Go ahead, though. I'll watch."

Drooping with disappointment, the little brush returned to its box as Aphrodite's brush began dusting sparkly blue powder on her eyelids.

It had been on the tip of Persephone's tongue to say that she'd watch too, but Aphrodite had already pulled out a stool for her and the third brush was hovering over her impatiently, waiting to begin. "Hop up," Aphrodite said. "This will be fun!"

Persephone obeyed, and the brush immediately began dusting blue on her eyelids as well.

When the goddessgirls finally left the shop, Aphrodite's and Persephone's eyes were heavily lined with black kohl, and Persephone carried a bagful of lipsticks, eyeliners, and eye powders that she didn't really want.

Oh well, she thought, she'd leave them in the Beautyology classroom later. She could hardly wait to wipe off the kohl from around her eyes when she got home. Against her already super-pale skin, the heavy black eyeliner made her look positively pasty. On Aphrodite, of course, the kohl looked great, but it made Persephone feel like a raccoon.

"Look!" Athena exclaimed. "There's Arachne's Sewing Supplies." The goddessgirls hurried over to the shop. Athena and Aphrodite oohed and aahed over bins of shimmery fabrics and colorful threads and yarns.

Aphrodite held up a length of sparkly pink fabric. "I want to make a new chiton for the dance on Friday," she said. "This will be perfect!"

"Yeah!" Persephone pretended to be excited too, but in truth she was bored. Besides, she didn't plan to go to the Harvest Hop. Even if she *had* wanted to go, she doubted her mom would let her. She thought Persephone was too young for dances—for any activity involving godboys, actually. Her mom owned a shop in the mall, Demeter's Daisies, Daffodils, and Floral Delights. Persephone would have enjoyed stopping by to see the new fall bouquets, but she didn't suggest it. She knew Athena and Aphrodite didn't share her interest in gardening.

"You should take up knitting, Persephone," said Athena. She held a big ball of luminescent green yarn next to Persephone's head. "What do you think?" she asked Aphrodite.

Aphrodite squinted at Persephone. "I think her hair could be less curly. Maybe a straightener—"

"I was asking about the color of the yarn next to her hair," interrupted Athena.

Leaping Olympians! thought Persephone, stunned. They were talking about her as if she wasn't even there! But she continued to stand between them as they tossed remarks about her back and forth over her head.

"Green goes perfect with red hair," Aphrodite declared. "And it heightens the green of her eyes. What are you thinking she should make? A cap?"

"But I—," Persephone started to protest.

"Don't worry," Athena interrupted again. "I invented a great pattern you can use."

Persephone sighed. She didn't want a cap. She *never* wore caps. Besides, despite having a green thumb for gardening, she was *all* thumbs at sewing and knitting. But faking an enthusiasm she didn't feel, she bought the yarn anyway, planning to return it next time she visited the market.

"Thanks," she told the saleslady in a cheerless voice. "I can't wait to use this." Her words sounded so false. Couldn't anyone else see what a phony she was? Even the sound of her name seemed to show it: PersePHONY. But she lacked the guts to say how she really felt about even the smallest things.

"Don't let me forget to give you that pattern later," Athena said as the goddessgirls left the mall.

Persephone nodded. "Sure," she said, though she rather hoped Athena *would* forget.

The three girls loosened the ties on their sandals to free the silver wings at their heels. The ties twined around their ankles again, and the wings began to flap. In seconds their sandals whisked them up the mountainside and through the clouds. When they were almost to the top of Mount Olympus, Persephone called out, "See you tomorrow!"

Waving, Athena and Aphrodite barely slowed as they ascended to the top of Mount Olympus without her. Persephone watched them wistfully. Among her friends, she was the only one who lived at home, instead of in the dorm.

Veering right, she came across a stream and washed off her eye makeup. Then, as she began to zip upward again, the papyrus bag holding her purchases ripped. The ball of yarn rolled out. She made a grab for it, but only just managed to catch the end of the string as the ball tumbled toward Earth, unwinding as it fell. "Come back here, you snarly little ball of trouble!" Persephone grumbled.

She followed it down, landing in a large open space of stony ground, patchy green grass, and scattered trees. *A park*, she thought. But then she noticed the rows and rows of gray stone markers and rectangular marble tombs. "Godness!" she exclaimed aloud. "It's a *cemetery*!"

2

Hades

PERSEPHONE HAD HEARD ABOUT CEMETERIES before, but until today she'd never actually seen one. By now, her yarn was strewn all over the rocky ground and caught on the tops of stone markers. She gathered the stringy stuff up and dropped the whole tangled mess into her chiton pocket. Then she took a good look around.

The cemetery covered an area as large as a stadium. Here and there, scraggly laurel and olive trees poked up through the ground like stray feathers on a plucked chicken. A gated stone wall surrounded the place, separating it from the town outside. *How odd,* Persephone thought, wondering why a wall was necessary. But maybe it was. Maybe mortals found the cemetery so inviting that *too many* were dying to get in. She giggled at her own joke.

Because she couldn't die—that's what it means to be immortal, after all—death had always fascinated Persephone. However, it wasn't a subject she discussed with her friends. The one time she *had* brought it up, they'd looked at her as if she were a stranger—and a *strange* stranger at that!

Persephone wandered through the cemetery, stopping

to admire the more elaborate monuments, including one with a marble bull perched on top. The plainer grave markers were simple stone cylinders, inscribed with the name of the deceased. Near the more recent of the graves, cups of wine and small cakes had been left as offerings to the spirits of the dead.

Next to one newly dug site, Persephone found some lilies scattered on the ground. She picked them up. Immediately the flowers' stalks straightened and became greener, and their drooping yellow petals curved upward, taking on a brighter hue. "That's better," she said to herself.

It was peaceful in the cemetery. Quite lovely, in fact. Persephone smiled. She was surprised how much at home she felt here. It was wonderful to have some alone time, with only her thoughts for company. She plucked a bunch of little daisies that had sprouted in a patch of grass. Relaxing against one of the stone markers, she began to weave a daisy chain.

Suddenly, not more than twenty feet away, the ground split open with a loud *crack*. "Yikes!" yelled Persephone. Her hands jerked and she dropped the daisy chain into her lap as a black stallion pushed up through the gap. It reared on its hind legs, and its front hooves pawed the air.

A godboy sat on the stallion's back. He seemed as startled to see Persephone as she was to see him. "Whoa!" he shouted. The stallion calmed, and the godboy nimbly leaped down. He swept back his hair, which hung in long, dusky ringlets. "I know you," he said coolly. "Persephone, right? I've seen you at school. What are you doing here in my cemetery?"

Persephone pulled part of the tangled pile of green string from her pocket. "I lost my ball of yarn. It fell out of my bag, and I followed it down here." She was surprised the godboy knew her name. He was older than her, maybe fourteen. He wasn't in any of her classes, but she did recall seeing him skulking along the hallways at school. Once she'd seen some mean godboys push him up against a wall. They'd been led by Ares, a real hothead.

The godboy was staring at her. He was cute in a dark and brooding sort of way, with flashing black eyes and a fine, straight nose. "What's your name?" Persephone asked, blushing under his steady gaze.

He raised an eyebrow, as if he was surprised—and maybe a little insulted—that she didn't already know. "Hades."

Persephone gave a little gasp. She'd heard his name before, and though she couldn't remember exactly what she'd heard, she knew it wasn't good. For one thing, Hades was from the *Underworld*—a gloomy, lonely, horrible place. Or that was the rumor, anyway. Yet he didn't *seem* horrible.

Frowning, Hades waved a hand toward the cemetery. "Most goddessgirls wouldn't step foot in a place like this. Doesn't it creep you out to be here?"

Persephone tossed her curly head. "Not a bit," she replied. "I like it here. It's peaceful."

Hades seemed pleased by her response. He nodded. "It *is* peaceful."

"Is this where you live? Or—" She glanced at the hole his horse had galloped out of.

"No, but I come here a lot. Especially when I need a

break from school and stuff." He sat beside her.

"Oh," said Persephone, hugging her knees. "I know what you mean. Sometimes I need to get away from things for a while too."

"I'm not real good at school," Hades confessed. He picked up a stick and dug at the ground with it. His dark hair fell over his brow.

"Me neither," Persephone lied. She was doing very well in her classes, but she didn't want Hades to feel bad.

"That's not true. I know you make As." He looked at her curiously. "Why are you lying?"

"Lying?" Persephone gulped. But he was right, and she liked that he had been so straightforward. She decided to be the same. "I guess I just wanted you to feel better."

He nodded, seeming to understand. "Sometimes I

skip classes when I don't want to go. Which is most of the time."

Persephone thought about saying that she sometimes skipped too, but stopped herself from telling another lie. She was sure Hades would see through it. Instead she said softly, "Maybe that's why you don't do real well in school."

He looked at her and laughed. "Yeah, maybe you're right."

"Do you have any classes with Mr. Cyclops?" Persephone asked as they continued to talk.

Hades nodded again. "I have him for my last class of the day."

"Does he walk around barefoot in your class too?" Persephone asked, giggling.

Still bent over his stick, Hades grinned. "Yes, and

he leaves his sandals lying around for everyone to trip over. Those things are as big as boats!"

Persephone nodded. "It's become a game to hide them."

"Have you ever done that?"

"No, but once, my friends Athena and Aphrodite decorated them with glittery stars and hung them from the ceiling!"

"I've seen you with them. Your friends," Hades said casually.

She'd been surprised that he knew her name, and that she got As, but the fact that he'd noticed her with her friends made Persephone feel happier than she'd felt all day. When it came to godboys, it was usually Aphrodite who drew all the attention. Blushing, she said, "Really? So who do you hang out with?"

Hades pushed on his stick so hard it broke in two. "I'm kind of a loner," he muttered darkly. Then, lightening up a little, he shot her a glance and said, "Tell me more about your friends."

Persephone would have liked to ask why he didn't pal around with the other godboys, but since it was obviously a sore subject, she was happy to talk about her friends instead. "Athena is so smart, she invented the olive," she said. "And no one knows more about fashion than Aphrodite. Then there's Artemis. She's the best archer in the Academy! And she has these three dogs. Once they got ahold of Mr. Cyclops's sandals. What a drooly mess—"

"I heard!" interrupted Hades, laughing again. Persephone liked the deep, rumbly sound of his voice. "I've got a dog too," he said. "Mine has three heads.

Cerberus. But he's a working dog. I can't bring him to school."

Persephone nodded. "Yeah, I've heard about him." He guarded the entrance to the Underworld and kept souls from escaping. She shivered just thinking about it. It seemed so creepy.

"So now tell me about you," Hades said. "What do *you* do best?"

"Well, I can garden a bit," said Persephone, surprised. Usually people liked to talk about themselves. It was weird to have someone ask about her. "My mom's Demeter."

"Goddess of the harvest and bringer of seasons, right?" said Hades.

"Yes," said Persephone.

"You take after her," said Hades.

"I can make things grow, anyway," said Persephone, shrugging.

"Show me," said Hades.

"Huh?"

"Show me how you can make things grow." He sat back, almost daring her, resting his weight on his hands.

"It's really not that big a deal," Persephone protested.

When he just stared at her with those dark eyes of his, she shrugged and reached into her lap for her daisy chain. By now all the little daisies had become limp. But as she held up the chain and gently stroked the flowers, their green stems and white petals straightened and grew strong again, as if they were still in the ground.

Hades' jaw dropped. "Cool! Where I come from almost

27

nothing grows—except asphodel. You've got skills!"

Persephone smiled. "Thanks." She couldn't imagine a place where things didn't grow. Asphodel was nice, though. She'd always liked the star-shaped white flowers, which grew atop tall stalks. Before she could ask Hades more about the Underworld, a chariot drawn by two wheat-colored horses swooped down from the sky.

"Oh, no—my mom!"

Beside her, she felt Hades stiffen. It was almost as if he'd learned to always expect trouble.

Demeter jumped down from the chariot as soon as it landed, and hustled over to Persephone. "I've been looking for you everywhere," she scolded. "You should've been home an hour ago. What are you doing in this awful place?" She herded Persephone onto the chariot. Then, whirling around, she gave Hades a look that would've killed if he hadn't already been immortal. "Stay away from my daughter, god-boy!" she warned him.

For a second, hurt flitted across Hades' face, but then his features hardened into an unreadable mask and he turned away.

"Mom!" Persephone's cheeks burned with embarrassment as the chariot lifted off.

Demeter urged the horses on. "If you don't like me hunting you down, you shouldn't wander off on your own without telling me where you're going and when you'll return," she replied as the chariot picked up speed.

Persephone tried to swallow the knot of anger that had become lodged in her stomach. It wasn't the first time her mom had come looking for her. In fact, Demeter was the ultimate chariot mom, racing here, there, and everywhere to keep tabs on her daughter. But whenever Persephone complained to her friends, Aphrodite said she should feel grateful she even *had* a mom. Having sprung from sea foam, Aphrodite had no parents at all. And Athena's mom was a fly! They just didn't understand.

"Who was that godboy, anyway?" Demeter demanded after a while. "I didn't like the look of him at all."

Persephone shrugged. "He didn't say," she lied.

Demeter pursed her lips, and they rode in silence a few minutes longer. At last she said, "Promise me you won't go off on your own again without telling me beforehand."

"Fine," Persephone said stonily. At times like this,

she couldn't help thinking that Aphrodite, Artemis, and Athena were fortunate not to have moms around. Feeling rebellious, she vowed to return to Earth as soon as possible. And with luck, she'd see Hades at school tomorrow.

3

The Missing Dandals

Although persephone looked for hades in the hallways at school the next morning, she didn't spot him. Maybe he was skipping classes again. What a letdown. She'd been so hoping to see him again.

Now, as she sat through a boring lecture in Mr. Cyclops's Hero-ology class, her third class of the day, she moodily toyed with her hair, pulling at a curl and letting it spring back.

She hadn't wanted to lie to her mom last night about knowing Hades' name. But if given that scrap of information, her mom would've pursued it like a bee after pollen. Demeter had always checked out Persephone's friends and never hesitated to criticize them. In *her* view, Aphrodite was too obsessed with her looks, Athena was too smart for her own good, and Artemis spent far too much time traipsing about in the woods with her dogs. It was a miracle Persephone was even allowed to *have* friends!

Since she wasn't paying attention, she was caught unawares when Mr. Cyclops asked her a question. "Could you repeat that?" she asked, sitting up straighter.

Her teacher rolled the single humongous eye in the middle of his forehead. "I asked if you knew where they went."

Where *who* went? Persephone's cheeks flushed. She hadn't a clue what he was talking about. She couldn't very well ask him to explain, though. Then he'd know for sure that she hadn't been listening.

"Well?" asked Mr. Cyclops, tapping an enormous bare foot.

"I'm thinking," said Persephone. He'd been talking about heroes, of course. He must have asked where they went after they died in battle. "Heaven?" she guessed.

The class roared with laughter.

Mr. Cyclops's huge eye blinked. "I asked if you knew where my sandals went. It would be quite amazing if they found their way to heaven." He paused. "Though, of course, they do have *soles*."

Everyone groaned at the pun. Why had Mr. Cyclops asked *her* about his sandals? Persephone wondered. Students were always hiding them. Even if she did know who had taken them this time, she wouldn't have told. She was no snitch.

A girl with short, spiky orange hair waved her hand in the air. It was Pheme, the goddess of gossip and rumor. "I heard that some godboys dragged them down to the River Styx to go rafting last night." As she spoke, words puffed from her lips like miniature smoke writing.

Snickers drifted over the class.

Mr. Cyclops sighed. "I'll make a deal. Whoever finds

my sandals and brings them back can skip the next two homework assignments."

Persephone's interest perked up. She wouldn't mind getting out of a couple of assignments. And looking for the sandals would give her an excuse to return to Earth. Maybe she'd see Hades again! She didn't need to tell her mom first either. Persephone had only promised not to go off *on her own.* She'd convince Aphrodite, Athena, and Artemis to go with her. If they did find the sandals, it would take all four of them to carry them back, anyway.

Ping! Ping! Ping! The lunch lyrebell sounded, and she headed for the cafeteria. The octopus-like lunch lady handed orange clay bowls decorated with black silhouetted figures to her and the next seven students in line. Persephone sniffed the contents appreciatively.

Mmmm. Yambrosia. She grabbed a carton of nectar from a tray and headed for the lunch table where she and her friends always sat together.

"Mr. Cyclops's sandals are missing," she said as she sat down. "Whoever finds them gets to—"

"—skip the next two homework assignments," finished Athena. As usual, a bag of scrolls lay on the bench beside her. She pushed a straw into her carton of nectar. "He's been asking about his sandals in all his classes, making the same offer to everyone. Aphrodite and I heard about it first period."

"And I found out during second period," said Artemis. She was still wearing her quiver of arrows, but she'd leaned her bow against the wall behind the table. At her feet lay her three dogs: a bloodhound, a greyhound, and a beagle. They followed her everywhere, even to class. She must have seen Persephone looking at them, because she said, "You don't mind, do you?"

The dogs *were* kind of smelly, but Persephone knew how much her friend adored them. "No, of course not."

Persephone quickly shared what Pheme had told her class about the sandals. "Of course, it's only a rumor."

"Most things she says are," said Artemis. "But it *might* be true." She set her half-empty bowl of yambrosia on the floor for her hounds to finish off. As usual, Amby, the beagle, beat the two older, bigger dogs to the bowl, gobbling down far more than his fair share. Running a hand through her short black hair, she said, "I think we should check it out at least. Missing two homework assignments would give me extra time to practice archery. There's a big contest coming up, and I want to be ready."

Athena's nose popped out of the plum-colored scroll she was reading. "I could use the time too. I'm swamped."

No surprise there, thought Persephone. Athena loved studying and had signed up for more than a full load of classes, plus some extracurriculars.

Aphrodite tossed back her beautiful golden hair. "Let's do it! Off to the river, then?"

Persephone smiled. Convincing her friends to join in the search had been easier than she'd expected. In fact, they'd convinced *themselves*. Now she just had to hope she'd see Hades!

4

The Search

T HAT AFTERNOON, BEFORE HEADING TO
Earth, the four friends made a quick stop at Aphrodite's dorm room so she could change into her "search
party" outfit. Persephone wasn't sure why a different
outfit was necessary, but the navy chiton, patterned
with little white sailing ships, certainly looked good

on Aphrodite. *Everything* did, of course.

On their way out of the dorm, the four friends grabbed winged sandals, then raced toward the River Styx. Its source was a spring that plunged down a rocky cliff high above them.

Unfortunately, Pheme's rumor had spread faster than fire on a windy day. *All* the godboys and goddess-girls from Mr. Cyclops's classes were out searching for the giant sandals along the river, the boundary between Earth and the Underworld.

A large eagle soared over Persephone's head to land at the river's edge. When the huge bird morphed into Ares, the goddessgirls nearby squealed with delight at the handsome godboy's arrival. Most gods and goddesses could shape-shift. Taking on the forms of animals at will was easy. Persephone herself often took the form of a dove when she flew places.

As the four goddessgirls skidded to a stop near the river, a golden-haired godboy with pale turquoise eyes and skin emerged from underwater with a triumphant grin on his face. Thrusting his three-pronged spear in the air, Poseidon exclaimed, "Found one! Someone's pinned it down to the riverbed with a boulder so it won't float!"

Persephone and all the other godboys and goddess-girls glanced suspiciously at Atlas. The academy's bulky champion weight lifter, he was likely the only godboy in the whole school capable of moving such a boulder.

Atlas shrugged. *Pheme was right*, thought Persephone. And Atlas must have been one of the godboys who had taken the sandals. Now he and Ares waded into

42

the water to help Poseidon bring up the one under the rock.

"Where's the second one?" Aphrodite shouted from shore.

Atlas raised both hands, palms up. "Don't know."

"It could have washed up near the riverbank," said Athena. "Why don't we spread out and search?"

Persephone moved toward some tall clumps of grass. Suddenly she heard a loud *crack* behind her. She whirled around. *Hades!* A blush stole across her cheeks as he emerged from the ground atop his stallion.

"Hi," he said, leaping down. "What's everyone looking for?"

"Haven't you heard?"

Hades' dark ringlets swung from side to side as he shook his head.

Then Persephone remembered that she hadn't seen him in school all day. Pointing to the sandal that Poseidon, Ares, and Atlas were now dragging toward shore, she explained about the reward Mr. Cyclops had offered.

Hades gave her a half smile. "Those things usually come in pairs, right?"

"Right," said Persephone. "Have you seen the other one?"

"Maybe," Hades teased.

"Show me," said Persephone.

Hades cocked his head. "What about your mom?"

Persephone sighed, feeling annoyed. "What about her?"

"I don't think she likes me." Hades' brow furrowed.

"She probably wouldn't like you going off with me—even to rescue a teacher's sandal."

Persephone pursed her lips in exasperation. "Ugh, my mom is always so worried! She probably thinks you'd *kidnap* me, given half a chance."

Before Hades could respond, Artemis ran up with her hounds at her heels. "Oh, *there* you are!" she said to Persephone. "Is this godboy giving you trouble?" She glared at Hades while her dogs stood at attention, their teeth bared.

"No, why would you think that?" Persephone replied. Then she noticed how tightly Artemis was clutching her bow. Hades' hands were balled into fists at his sides, and his feet were planted wide as if he expected an attack.

"Godness!" Persephone exclaimed, stepping between

them. "Relax, Hades. Artemis is my friend."

She turned toward Artemis. "I don't need protection. Hades is a friend too."

"If you say so," Artemis growled. Her grip on her bow relaxed, but she continued to glare at Hades. Her dogs growled and glared too.

Moments later Aphrodite and Athena also ran up. Sandwiching Persephone, they slipped their arms through hers. Aphrodite arched an eyebrow at Hades. In a frosty voice, she said, "So sorry, but Persephone has to go now."

Before Persephone could protest, the two goddess-girls practically dragged her away. Artemis followed with her dogs. When she overcame her shock, Persephone began to struggle, but Athena and Aphrodite held on. "Keep walking," Aphrodite said sternly.

Persephone twisted her head to look over her shoulder, but Hades had already disappeared. She scowled at her so-called friends. "Why are you doing this?" Then her eyes narrowed with suspicion and she groaned. "Don't tell me. My mom put you up to this, didn't she?"

5

The Second Sandal

APHRODITE AND ATHENA LOOSENED THEIR
hold on Persephone. "Your mom?" Aphrodite asked
blankly.

Persephone frowned. "Yes, my mom. It's just the
kind of thing she would do. She's as overprotective as
a suit of armor. Hades and I are friends—at least, we
were starting to be."

Athena snorted. "Demeter has nothing to do with this."

"It was our idea," Artemis agreed. "You *cannot* be friends with Hades."

Persephone's eyes widened. "Why not?"

"Because," Aphrodite said, speaking slowly and clearly, "he's from the *Underworld*."

"So?" said Persephone. "Just because someone comes from the wrong side of the world, it doesn't mean they aren't worth knowing."

Athena nodded. "True. But Hades is trouble with a capital *T*! Everyone says so."

"Well, *I* don't believe it," Persephone said stubbornly.

The goddessgirls climbed to the top of a hill overlooking the river. "Anyway," Persephone added, "he was about to show me where Mr. Cyclops's other sandal is hidden."

Just then shouts came from below. The four goddess-girls looked down. Pheme had found the second sandal. After an impromptu celebratory dance, she hoisted it over her spiky orange head with the help of two other goddessgirls.

Artemis eyed Persephone. "You were saying?" she said dryly.

Persephone blushed. "He must have shown Pheme where it was hidden instead." But though she scanned the faces near Pheme several times, she didn't see Hades.

Aphrodite shook her head. "We're your friends, Persephone. Take our advice. Stay away from Hades. He may be cute in a gloomy kind of way, but he's bad news."

Persephone opened her mouth to defend him again, but then she closed it. What if her friends and her mom were right? What if Hades had lied about showing her where the other giant sandal was? How well did she *really* know him?

By the time the goddessgirls returned to Mount Olympus and Persephone arrived home, she'd decided her gut feelings about Hades must have been wrong. After all, how could she be right about him when everyone else thought differently? Still, she felt sad to have to end their budding friendship.

Arriving at school the next day, Persephone crossed the courtyard and began to climb the wide granite steps to the bronze doors of the academy. She was halfway up when Hades stepped from behind a tall pillar and came toward her. Persephone pretended not to see him and swerved to avoid him. Spotting Athena and her mortal roommate, Pandora, she raced to catch up with them.

"Where did you come from?" Pandora asked right away. Gold streaks in her blue hair glinted in the sunlight. And because she was mortal, she didn't have shimmery skin like Persephone and the other immortals. "You were down at the River Styx yesterday, weren't you? Do you think someone will take Mr. Cyclops's sandals again?"

Persephone didn't bother to reply, knowing it wasn't necessary. With Pandora, it was impossible to get a word in edgewise anyway. Sure enough, the girl quickly turned her questions back to Athena. As if a symbol of her constant curiosity, Pandora's bangs clung to her forehead in the shape of a question mark.

On her way to Mr. Cyclops's class, Persephone saw Hades again. He was skulking along the hallway wearing a scowl. When he glimpsed her, however, his face lit up.

Ducking her head, Persephone raced across the hall and escaped into Mr. Cyclops's classroom. Just inside the door, she tripped over one of his sandals. This time, though, his foot was actually in it. "*Some-one's* in a hurry," he said. He plucked her from the floor as if she were a flower and set her upright on her stems.

"Thanks," she said.

Mr. Cyclops's enormous eye winked at her. "I think

it's great that you just couldn't wait to be in class."

Persephone sighed as she took her seat. He obviously didn't have a clue about the problems she had to deal with!

Later, as she stood in line for lunch, she looked nervously around for Hades. Fortunately, she didn't see him. Come to think of it, though, she'd *never* seen him in the cafeteria. He must eat lunch somewhere else—probably by himself, since he didn't seem to have any friends. The thought made her feel a bit guilty for avoiding him, but what else could she do?

Persephone accepted her steaming bowl of nectaroni and cheese from the eight-armed lunch lady. Then she headed for her three friends at their usual table. They were talking animatedly until she drew near. Then they exchanged glances and fell silent. Her friends must have been talking about *her*! It kind of hurt her feelings.

"So how is everyone today?" she asked in a fake, sunny voice as she sat down.

"Good, thanks," said Aphrodite.

Artemis and Athena nodded. "And how are *you?*" asked Artemis.

"Fabulous," Persephone said brightly. "Couldn't be better." They all looked relieved. No one seemed to notice the false note in her voice.

Athena was eyeing Persephone's bowl. "Would you mind trading?" she asked. "The nectaroni and cheese was gone when I went through the line. I'm not that fond of ambrosia chowder."

Neither was Persephone, but she let Athena trade with her anyway. As she dipped her spoon into the too-sweet chowder, she thought sadly that things had returned to normal. Once again she was going along to get along. Once again she'd slipped into being Perse-PHONY.

Athena began to talk about something funny that had happened in her second-period class involving Pandora and a two-headed godboy, but Persephone tuned out. Her thoughts returned to the cemetery, with its grand stone monuments and its peaceful air. Was it really only two days ago that she'd first discovered the place? She smiled to herself, remembering how startled she'd been when Hades emerged from below the earth on the back of his great black stallion. But of course, he'd been startled to see her, too.

Later, when the lyrebell sounded the end of the

lunch period, Aphrodite turned to her. "Any after-school plans today?" she asked lightly. "Want to go shopping again?"

Oh, no! thought Persephone. *Shopping again?* But, much as she disliked the idea, she really didn't have any other plans. She was about to go along as usual when she noticed that all three of her friends were looking at her intently, waiting for her answer.

They're worried that if I say no, I'll go see Hades again instead! she realized. Anger burned inside her. She felt like she'd swallowed a lit coal. How *dare* they try to control her life! Why, they were as bad as her mom. "No, thanks," she said crisply. "I have something else to do." Her friends could think what they wanted!

Rising abruptly, she left the table, hurrying away

before anyone could ask what her plans were. Truth was, she didn't even know herself. As she marched out of the cafeteria and down the hall to her next class, Persephone smiled to herself. This time it was a *genuine* smile. It was amazing how good her tiny act of rebellion had made her feel.

6

Pomegranate Deeds

By the time the school day was over, Persephone knew what she wanted to do. She would visit the cemetery again. Holding on to an image of a dove in her mind, she felt her arms turn to wings and her body grow lighter. When the change was complete, she fluttered toward Earth. Just before she reached the cemetery, she came upon a pomegranate orchard.

Unable to resist the sweet fruit, she changed back to her goddess form and picked the biggest, juiciest pomegranate she could find. Then, cupping her prize in both hands, she walked the rest of the way to the cemetery.

Persephone looked around for Hades, but he wasn't there. Unsure whether she should feel disappointed or relieved, she split open the pomegranate against a gravestone and settled onto the grass to enjoy her favorite fruit.

It was nice being by herself. There was no one here to tell her what to do and who to see or not see. She sucked the sweet, juicy pulp from around each pomegranate seed, then spat them out, challenging herself to see how far she could send them flying.

Suddenly the ground cracked open in front of her and Hades appeared astride his stallion. Startled,

Persephone swallowed the seed she was planning to spit next.

Hades jumped down from his horse. "Why did you come back?" he said, scowling at her.

She gulped, feeling embarrassed. She'd wanted to see him. Why was he acting so sorry to see her? "I told you before, I like it here," she said.

Hades glowered at her. "Didn't you think *I* might turn up?"

"So?" Persephone stuck out her chin.

"You were avoiding me at school today," he said in an accusing voice.

So that *was it*, thought Persephone. She'd hoped he hadn't noticed. "Look, I'm sorry about that." She held half of her pomegranate out to him like a peace offering. "Want some? It's delicious."

When he hesitated, she smiled, adding, "We could have a seed-spitting contest."

At her smile, his bad mood seemed to melt away. "A spitting contest?"

"Sure."

He flashed her a grin. "You're on."

Persephone picked up some fallen twigs and laid them end-to-end on the lawn. Then she stood behind the line she'd created. Using her tongue and the roof of her mouth, she rolled a seed into position, then spat. *Ptooey!* It flew out of her mouth and landed a good eighteen feet away.

"Hey, you're pretty good! But it's my turn now," Hades said, wiggling his brows in a teasing way. He planted himself on the line, and a look of concentration settled on his face. Puffing up his cheeks, he blew, rather than spat, the seed out. It plopped in the dirt at his feet. He stared at the seed with a look of grave disappointment. "This is harder than I thought."

Persephone stifled a giggle. "Want some advice?"

"Sure," said Hades, looking back at her.

He had the most beautiful eyes, she thought, as black and intense as smoldering coals. And it was nice that he didn't get all huffy because a girl had beaten him. "First you have to roll the seed into position." As she demonstrated, he watched her closely. She felt herself flush under his scrutiny.

But then he popped another seed in his mouth. "Like thith?" he said, his tongue pushing the seed against the roof of his mouth.

"That's it!" said Persephone, trying not to laugh. It was impossible to look dignified when spitting seeds.

"Now tilt your head up and blow hard. You need to get some air behind that seed."

This time Hades managed to send his seed a foot farther than before. As he continued to practice, Persephone glanced up and saw three hawks circling low in the sky. One had a black stripe on top of its head, another had golden feathers, and the third was lustrous brown. She wondered if they were hunting for birds or rabbits. They swooped overhead a few times, then finally flew away.

After a few more tries, Hades' seed spitting improved, but there was no way he could outspit Persephone. "You win," he said finally. He flopped onto the ground, and she sat beside him. "Know something?" he said, glancing sideways at her from under thick eyelashes. "I really like you. You're the first goddessgirl

I've met who isn't freaked out just because I'm from the Underworld."

Persephone's heart gave a little flutter. She was surprised how much his words touched her. "It shouldn't matter where someone's from," she said.

"Agreed," said Hades. "But most goddessgirls pretty much shun me." His eyes slid away from hers. "Your friends dragged you off fast enough when they saw you with me at the river yesterday."

"I know," Persephone said softly. She took a deep breath. "They say you're bad news." She was taking a risk being so honest, but somehow she felt he was the kind of friend who might understand.

A dark shadow passed over his face. For a moment Persephone worried she'd misjudged. But then he sighed. "Do you know why they say that?"

She was surprised to realize that she didn't, and shook her head. "No, I never asked."

Hades shrugged. "I don't know either." He paused. "I do spend a lot of time in Principal Zeus's office. Pheme saw me in there once, and I think she may have spread the word that I'm in trouble a lot."

Persephone nodded. Pheme could well be the source of Hades' bad rap. "Why do you spend so much time in the office?" she asked.

"Because Principal Zeus is cool."

"Cool?"

"Yeah. I mean, have you ever talked to the guy?"

"No, he's kind of scary."

"That's what I used to think too. I guess it would be hard *not* to be intimidated by someone who's King of the Gods and Ruler of the Heavens, on top of being principal of the academy. But I know what it's like to be judged unfairly, so I gave him a chance. Once I got past the fact that he's huge, speaks in a voice like thunder, and causes an electric shock every time he shakes my hand, I discovered he's a really great guy."

"So you hang out in his office?" Persephone asked, fascinated.

"I think he heard that some of the godboys give me a hard time." Hades paused, looking pained, and she wondered what awful experiences he was remembering. "So he invited me to eat lunch with him in his office every day," he went on. "Sometimes I study there too. Or we talk."

He *talked* to Principal Zeus? She hardly knew anyone

brave enough to go near him, much less talk to him. Except, of course, Athena. But then, Zeus was her *dad*.

"So what do you talk about?"

"Stuff." As if he were a little embarrassed he'd told her so much about himself, he seemed to suddenly close up tighter than a brand-new bud.

Well, that explains the rumors, anyway, thought Persephone. She was glad her gut feeling about Hades had been right after all. Still . . . "Did you really know where Mr. Cyclops's other sandal was—the one Pheme found?"

"Yep," said Hades, shooting her a look. "Didn't believe me, huh? I did, though. It washed up in the Underworld. I wanted to give it to you, but in the meantime Charon found it and towed it upriver."

Persephone nodded. "I see." She knew about Charon. He was the old man who ferried the dead across the River Styx to the Underworld. Glancing up at the sky, she noticed that the sun was getting low. She jumped up. "I'd better go. My mom will come looking for me again if I don't get home soon."

Hades stood too. "I'd hate for you to get in trouble on my account," he said. "I don't usually talk so much, but—" He spread his hands, looking almost shy. "You're so easy to talk to."

Persephone smiled. "You too. See you at school tomorrow." Quickly she changed into a dove and flew up the mountainside, darting through the clouds to the top of Mount Olympus.

"Hi, Mom, I'm home!" she called out as she entered the house. There was no reply. She heard voices. Her mom must have guests.

Persephone wandered down the hallway to the courtyard. Then she stopped short. Her jaw dropped as her three friends and her mom whipped around to look at her. "How could you?" Demeter scolded. "I trusted you to keep your word!"

Like a willow tree, Persephone stood rooted to the spot as her mom's words rained down on her. She couldn't believe it. Her friends must have *told* on her. But how had they known? Then she remembered the three hawks circling overhead—one with a black streak, one with golden tail feathers, and one brown . . . the goddessgirls in disguise! They hadn't been hunting for birds or rabbits after all. They'd been hunting for *her*.

"You have no idea of the dangers in the world," Demeter ranted on. "Why, you could have gotten lost. You could've hurt yourself. You could've been abducted!"

"How could *I*? How could *you*?!" Persephone cried, her shock turning to anger. She glanced at her friends, but none met her eye. Were they embarrassed for her? Suddenly the public humiliation was more than she could bear. Turning, she bolted down the hall to her room. Tears of hurt and anger streamed down her face. With friends like hers, who needed enemies?

7

In the Underworld

AFTER A WHILE SOMEONE KNOCKED LIGHTLY on Persephone's door. "Can I come in?"

It was Aphrodite. "Go away!" Persephone yelled.

"Please," Aphrodite called through the door. "We need to talk."

"I don't want to. Not now, not ever!"

"It's not like you think," Aphrodite protested. "We were worried about you. And your mom practically *made* us tell her. We didn't mean to get you in trouble."

"Right," Persephone said sarcastically. "Well, thanks for nothing!"

There was a pause, and she could hear whispers. Athena and Artemis must be outside her door too. At last Aphrodite spoke again. "You're not yourself right now," she said. "We'll talk to you at school tomorrow after you've calmed down, okay?"

Persephone didn't answer. Moments later she heard her friends leave. Aphrodite had it all wrong, she thought. This angry self *was* her real self. The Persephone her friends thought they knew, the one who went along to get along, was the *phony* Persephone.

From now on that Persephone was gone forever!

Demeter made yambrosia for dinner that night. Although the school's yambrosia was good, her mom's was *heavenly*. Persephone knew it was an attempt to patch things up between them, but she stubbornly ate her bowlful in silence and stared down at the tabletop to avoid looking at her mom. The only sound during the meal was the clicking of spoons against their ceramic bowls.

Later, as they were doing the washing up before bedtime, Demeter set down her dishcloth and sighed. "I'm sorry. I know I shouldn't have scolded you in front of your friends this afternoon."

Persephone grunted but didn't reply.

"You're my only daughter," her mom continued. "I don't know what I'd do if I lost you."

74

Breaking her silence at long last, Persephone muttered, "I'm not something you can misplace. I'm not a turquoise ring or an emerald bracelet."

Her mom frowned. "Don't get smart with me. You know what I mean." In a calmer voice she said, "It's late. We'll talk more tomorrow." Taking a step toward Persephone, she added, "Good night." As her mom bent to kiss her, Persephone turned her cheek away. "See you in the morning," Demeter said softly. Then she headed down the hall to her room.

Persephone knew she'd hurt her, but she shoved away her feelings of guilt. If she forgave her mom now, she'd simply fall back into her old pattern of letting others tell her how to behave, and that was something she was determined *not* to do.

Returning to her room, she paced back and forth

on the mosaic floor tiles beside her bed, thinking about what had happened and what she should do next. She just *couldn't* continue to be the goddessgirl her friends and her mom thought she was. And then, like a bolt of lightning from Zeus, an idea struck her. She would run away!

And she knew exactly where she'd go.

Once she was sure Demeter was asleep, Persephone packed a few chitons and other things she'd need into a woven bag and sneaked out of the house. Hesitating on the doorstep, she looked back for one long moment. It wasn't too late to return to her room. She could still change her mind. Feeling her resolve waver, she steeled her spine. Then she clutched her bag tightly and hurried away.

Since Hades was her only *real* friend, she'd decided

to ask him if she could stay at his place. Turning herself into a dove, she grabbed her bag in her beak and dropped down to the River Styx. About a half mile past the spot where Mr. Cyclops's sandals had been found, she spied some shades—human souls—boarding Charon's boat for the trip to the Underworld.

Changing herself into an old woman, a favorite disguise of her mom's, Persephone joined the throng at the river's edge. Her body was solid compared to that of the wispy shades, but she hoped no one would notice. She waited until it was her turn, then approached Charon. "I'd like passage to the Underworld, please," she said.

Raising his grizzled chin, he looked her up and down. Persephone pulled her brown woolen shawl tighter. For a moment she worried that the stooped old ferryman would see through her disguise, but all he said was, "That'll be one obol, please."

Persephone stared at him, dumbfounded. She had no human money! Giving her an impatient look, Charon reached past her and plucked another's coin, and then pulled the soul onboard.

As Persephone found herself pushed aside in line, a shade with a gaunt body and a long beard leaned forward and tapped her on the shoulder. "You're not from around here, are you?" he whispered. "An obol is one sixth of a drachma."

"Thanks," she said. "But I don't have any coins— none at all."

"That's okay," said the shade. "I have an extra. Maybe helping you will bring me good fortune." He dropped a silver coin into the palm of her hand.

Persephone smiled. "You're very kind." If she had anything to say about it, this nice shade would get to stay in the Elysian Fields. She'd heard it was the Underworld's most desirable neighborhood and that those lucky enough to go there feasted, played, and sang forevermore. She handed Charon the coin and he helped her onto his boat, grunting and frowning at her unexpected weight.

When the shades were all onboard, Charon dipped his ferryman's pole into the river and shoved off from shore. As the boat glided away, a cold lump of fear settled to the bottom of Persephone's stomach. Clutching her bag to her chest, she thought how little she knew about the Underworld, after all. What had she gotten herself into? *Have courage,* she told herself. But what if her mom was right about the dangers of the world?

Surely the Underworld was the most fearsome place of all!

After a while the river branched into a swamp. Charon guided his boat to the far side until the craft bumped up against shore. "We're here. Everybody off!" he called out.

There was some grumbling among the shades, and a little pushing and shoving, as everyone left the boat. Trembling a little, Persephone climbed over the side.

She followed the shades as they filed past an enormous dog with three slobbering heads and a snakelike tail. *Cerberus!* she realized with excitement. Because she knew he was Hades' pet, he didn't seem frightening at all.

Cerberus lay with his heads on his paws, not bothering to look up as the shades entered the Underworld.

Persephone was tempted to reach out and pat him, but she didn't. She was afraid he might sniff out her disguise. But he ignored her, too. She knew it was his duty to keep souls from leaving, so he probably didn't care who came in as long as no one got *out.*

Following the shades, Persephone descended into the land of the dead. A dank, gray mist swallowed them up as they trudged down a marshy trail. Her sandals made sucking sounds as they sank into stagnant water that smelled of rotting grasses.

"Yuck," muttered the shade just ahead of her. "Could this place be any gloomier?"

It *was* a gloomy place all right, but Persephone didn't mind. Right now, it suited her mood.

After a while the mist cleared and the group came upon fields of asphodel. The tall stalks, topped with white blossoms, spread out in all directions. This part of the Underworld was rather nice, thought Persephone. So what if asphodel was the only flower that bloomed here? She bent down and sniffed the flowers' sweet fragrance. *Ahhh*. She *loved* asphodel.

So did the dead. Up ahead, some of them were even *eating* it. Squatting near the ashes of a fire, they toasted the roots before gobbling them down. Out in the fields, other shades harvested the blossoms. They moved about in a mechanical fashion, seeming neither happy nor unhappy. Just calm. Persephone felt that way too. Like she could be herself here.

Persephone looked around for Hades but didn't see him. He wouldn't be easy to find in such a large place. Well, she'd just have to keep looking. As the shades from the boat headed to a spot where three roads crossed, Persephone sneaked away from the group.

"Hey, where are you going, shade?" called a bearded man with wings attached to his shoulders. "We're just about ready to start the judging. You need to find out where you'll be placed." He studied a scroll list and then eyed her. "Do you mind fire?"

"Actually," Persephone admitted, "I'm not a shade at all. I'm a goddess in disguise. I—"

The bearded man raised an eyebrow. "If you're a goddess, I'm a Cyclops. Now get back in line."

"You don't understand. I'm only here to look for Hades," Persephone continued. "You see, I've run away from home and—"

"Is that so?" interrupted the bearded man, making

a quick note on his list. "Tsk-tsk. *That's* not going to increase your chances of getting into the Elysian Fields!"

"Hey, Thanatos!" Another bearded man with a scroll came up to them. The two men looked so much alike that Persephone guessed they must be twins. "There's some kind of trouble down in Tartarus," the second man said. "Hades volunteered to check it out. In the meantime, how about escorting a batch of shades up to the Palace?"

Thanatos frowned. "Why should I? I'm busy, Hypnos." He jabbed at his scroll list, as if to prove his point.

"You're not the only one who's overworked." Hypnos shook his scroll in Thanatos's face.

"Oh, yeah?"

"Yeah."

The two men glared at each other.

Persephone didn't wait to hear more. As the twins continued to bicker, she sneaked away.

Tartarus was said to be the worst place in the Underworld. It was where the truly evil wound up, including those who had offended the gods and goddesses. But if Hades was there, that's where she'd go. Her heart thumped in her chest as she tiptoed past the line of people waiting to be judged. She was sure that at any moment Thanatos or some other Underworld employee would come running after her. When no one did, she breathed a sigh of relief. Seeing a sign for Tartarus with an arrow pointing left, she set off in that direction, walking fast.

As she turned a corner, she screeched to a halt. She'd almost tumbled into a river of fire! At her feet, red-hot lava hissed and steamed as it flowed over jagged rocks. Great billowing clouds of gray smoke hung over the river, and the air stank of rotten eggs. Pinching her nose, Persephone shrank away from the waves of intense stink and heat that rose from the water. She followed the river as the ground sloped steeply downward. Tartarus was the lowest level of the Underworld, so at least she knew she was still headed in the right direction.

Eventually she came to an enormous lake that churned with boiling water and mud. Shades bobbed around in its bubbling waters, writhing and scream-ing. Suddenly she wasn't sure whether to hold her hands over her ears or her nose!

Shuddering, she wondered what these poor crea-tures had done to deserve such punishment. Surely something much worse than running away from home.

Seeing her reflection in a puddle along the shore, Persephone remembered that she still wore her crone disguise. After shedding it, her step quickened as she thought about seeing Hades. Even the trouble with her mom and her friends couldn't spoil the memories of how wonderful it had been to be with him yesterday. Eventually she came to the edge of a gaping pit. She stared down into it, but it was so deep she couldn't see the bottom. This must be the entrance to Tartarus!

As her eyes grew accustomed to the dimness here, she saw there were steps carved in the cavern's steep sides. Slinging her bag over her back, she began to climb down. The deeper she went, the danker the air became, and a murky gloom hung over the pit. She passed many shades along the way, each one more miserable than the last. They wrung their hands and thrashed about, complaining to whomever would listen that their being here was all a mistake.

"I was *framed*," one shouted to her when he noticed her. "And anyway, even if I did take the food and money, I needed it more than those orphans!"

"It was an accident," another claimed. "The knife just sort of slipped from my hands. I don't know how it wound up in his back!"

Persephone might have pitied them if she hadn't doubted their truthfulness. Ignoring their feeble excuses, she called out, "Can any of you tell me where to find Hades?"

"You a friend of his?" the shade who claimed to have been framed asked eagerly.

"Yes."

"Put in a good word for me, and I'll tell you exactly where to find him," he said.

"Don't listen to him," another shade called out. "He doesn't know a thing. I'll help you find Hades, though. And as a return favor—"

"They're both liars," interrupted a third shade. "They have no idea where Hades has got to. But me and him are old pals, and . . ."

It seemed obvious that these shades would be of no help, so Persephone continued on down. After a while, she passed a shade rolling a large boulder up the side of the pit. But well before he reached the top, the boulder rolled back down again. He had to run after it to stop it, then start all over again. Persephone watched him a few times, shaking her head. He'd never get that rock to the top, and that was the point, she realized. As punishments went, it was an interesting one, but not terribly creative. She thought she could think up a better one for him if she knew why he was here.

It took forever to reach the bottom, but at last she arrived and immediately spotted Hades. She waved to him. He saw her and headed toward her. He looked worried. "What are you doing here?" he asked as they came even.

Persephone's face fell. She had thought he'd be happy to see her. "I ran away from home," she told him.

"Why?"

She stared at him. He must know that *he* was part of the reason—that no one liked her seeing him. But she couldn't quite bring herself to tell him that. Instead she said, "Because everyone keeps telling me what to do. I just couldn't stand it anymore!"

Hades raised an eyebrow. "Everyone?"

"Well, my mom and my friends." She told him what had happened when she got home from the cemetery.

Hades listened quietly. But when she had finished, he gently took her arm and stepped past her, trying to lead her from the pit. "You can't stay here. This is no place for someone like you."

Persephone yanked away and stood facing him. "Why not?"

"Because it's gloomy!" he explained, sounding frustrated and a little angry that she didn't seem to understand. "You're bright and sunny."

She scowled and crossed her arms. "Not always. Sometimes I just *pretend* to be."

Hades planted his hands on his hips. "Look, if your mom discovers you're gone, she'll be furious. Especially if she finds out you came here. To see me. Let me take you home."

"Why are you sticking up for *her*?" Persephone exclaimed. "You know she doesn't like you. And my friends don't either!"

"I'm used to it," Hades said grimly, but she thought he looked a little hurt. "Listen, it's not that I don't want you here. In fact, I'd like us to be friends. But if they find you here, your mom and the other goddessgirls will blame me. They'll like me even less than they do now. If that's possible."

Persephone knew Hades spoke the truth, but it was annoying that he wouldn't go along with her plan. Her face was a dark cloud as he called up his chariot and four black stallions. She stared stonily ahead when he escorted her out of the Underworld in the chariot, back across the River Styx, and up Mount Olympus. "You can leave me here," she said coldly when they drew near her home. "I'll *walk* the rest of the way."

Hades pulled back on the reins, and his stallions came to a halt. With a firm grip on her woven bag, Persephone hopped off the back of the chariot.

Hades grabbed her arm and waited till she looked at him. "See you at school."

She glared at him and pulled away. "Not if I see you first!" Ignoring the shocked look on his face, she stalked toward home.

8

Home Again

ALL WAS DARK AND QUIET AS PERSEPHONE
sneaked in the front door of her home. Tiptoeing, she
groped her way down the hall. But as she passed her
mom's door, she stubbed her toe on a loose mosaic tile.
"Ow!" she cried out. Dropping her bag, she hopped
about in pain.

"Persephone?" In a flash Demeter was out of bed

and at her daughter's side. Under a circle of lamplight, her golden hair shone and stuck out at odd angles. She'd thrown on her rosebud-patterned bathrobe in such a hurry that it was inside out. "What happened? Are you okay?" she asked worriedly.

"I'm fine." Persephone's heart beat wildly as she waited for her mom to ask why she was out of bed in the middle of the night.

"What's the matter? Couldn't you sleep?" asked Demeter. Then her gaze fell on Persephone's bag. Her forehead wrinkled. "What's that doing here?"

"I—um—" Persephone stopped, unwilling to lie, but unwilling to tell the truth, either.

Demeter's hand flew to her throat. "You were planning to run away, weren't you?"

Persephone rubbed her stubbed toe, looking away.

"Not planning to. Already *did*. But Hades made me come back home."

"I thought I smelled smoke!" wailed Demeter. "That horrible godboy! This was his idea, right? I can't believe you ran away to the Underworld! I—"

"Stop!" Persephone exclaimed. "You're not listening! It was *my* idea to run away, not Hades'."

Demeter turned as pale as a shade. "But why?"

"Because I was mad." Persephone let out a long sigh. "Can we sit down? I'm really tired. And my toe hurts."

"Yes, of course," her mom said. "Let's go to the kitchen. I'll get you a snack. And some cold water to soak your foot." In the kitchen, Demeter set some breadstyx and a bowl of nectar on the table.

"Thanks." Persephone sank onto a chair. Her mother set a bowl of cold water on the floor, and Persephone lowered her foot into it. Then she picked up one of the styx and dipped it into the nectar. When she was younger, her mom had often fixed this snack for her—especially whenever she'd woken from a nightmare in the middle of the night.

Demeter sat down across from her. "So tell me. Why did you run away?" she asked again. There was a pained look on her face. "Am I such a terrible mother?"

"No," said Persephone. "Of course not. I told you. I was just mad."

"I know you think I'm a chariot mom," Demeter said softly, "but I have more experience of the world than you. I know what can happen. It's my duty to protect you, even when you don't think you *need* protection."

"But I'm almost thirteen years old!" Persephone protested. "I can look after myself!"

"You *think* you can," Demeter said sharply. "But sometimes you don't use the best judgment."

Persephone bristled. She knew what her mom was thinking. "You're wrong about Hades!" she exclaimed. "So are my friends! Like I told you, he *made* me come home. In fact, he brought me back here. He knew you'd be upset if you found out I'd run away. He said I didn't belong in his world."

Demeter gaped at her. "He really said all that?"

Persephone nodded. She didn't tell her mom how mad she'd been at him for saying it, though. With a start she realized that this new, angry, daring side of her was no more *real* than the Persephone that went along to get along. The real her was somewhere in between.

Her eyes pleaded with her mom as she said, "How

can I get better at making judgments if you won't let me make my own?"

Demeter opened her mouth, and then closed it again. At last she sighed. "I guess you're right. I *do* need to give you more independence."

"Really?" Persephone's heart skipped a beat.

Demeter nodded. "It's hard for me to admit this, but you *are* getting older." She looked a little sad, and tears pricked her eyes. "You're not my little goddessgirl anymore."

Overwhelmed with love for her mother, Persephone took her foot out of the bowl of cold water and rose from the table. "Don't worry," she said, hugging her mom. "I'll always be your little goddessgirl—no matter how old I get."

* * *

As good as Persephone felt about her late-night talk with her mom, she was worried the next morning as she crossed the courtyard and began to climb the wide granite steps to the school. Would her friends be mad at her? Yesterday was the first time they'd ever seen her angry. What if they'd only liked her because she always tried to be nice?

"Persephone! Wait up!" Athena bounded toward her, with Aphrodite and Artemis right behind her.

"Hi," Persephone said awkwardly as they caught up to her.

"Hi," they said back.

For an awkward moment all four goddessgirls stood there silently. Finally Persephone looked away. "I'm sorry I—"

"We're sorry we—," Aphrodite started to say at the same time.

Both goddessgirls stopped talking. They smiled at each other. Then all four began to laugh.

"I'm so glad you're not mad at me," said Persephone.

"Us too," said Aphrodite.

"Yeah," Artemis and Athena agreed together.

Persephone could hardly believe it. Her friends must feel as bad about what had happened yesterday as she did!

"Are things okay between you and your mom?" Artemis asked anxiously as the friends linked arms and climbed to the top of the steps.

Persephone nodded. "We had a good talk last night."

"That's great!" said Athena.

Aphrodite studied Persephone. "I've never seen you as mad as you were yesterday." She grinned. "I didn't know you had it in you!"

"You erupted like a volcano," Athena added. "A real Mount Vesuvius!"

Persephone's cheeks burned. "I'm sorry."

"Don't be," said Artemis. "Don't you think *we* get angry sometimes too?"

Persephone thought for a moment. Then she remembered how mad Aphrodite had been at Artemis one day when her dogs got into Aphrodite's room and chewed up her favorite pair of sandals. And Artemis had practically gone ballistic once when Athena had beaten her in what was supposed to have been a friendly archery contest.

Yes, of course her friends got angry sometimes, she realized. Then it dawned on her: Strong friendships could survive an occasional outburst or bad mood. She didn't need to fear losing her friends. "From now on I promise not to keep my real feelings a secret," she said. Then she grinned. "So watch out!"

The goddessgirls laughed. As they passed between two Ionic columns and entered the school, Persephone told them about Hades being friends with Principal Zeus and how they ate lunch together most days. She was eager to put the "bad boy" rumors to rest. Then maybe her friends would see Hades in a new light.

When Persephone finished explaining, Aphrodite looked thoughtful. "Typical of Pheme to jump to conclusions," she said. "But we shouldn't have been so quick to believe her."

"True," said Artemis, "but it doesn't exactly help that Hades glowers all the time."

"Maybe we would too, if we had to live in the Under-world," said Athena.

"Actually, it's a rather interesting place," said Perse-phone, as they all paused in front of her locker.

Her friends stared at her, shocked looks on their faces. "You've been there?" asked Aphrodite.

Persephone nodded. "Last night, actually." She paused. "I ran away from home."

"What?" her friends exclaimed together.

So Persephone told them how she'd slipped out of the house, flown to Earth, then boarded Charon's boat disguised as an old woman. As she described how she'd trudged down a marshy trail, through fields of asphodel, along a river of fire, and down into the pit of

Tartarus past the shades of murderers and thieves, her friends' eyes widened.

"Ye gods!" Athena exclaimed. "Weren't you scared?"

"A little," Persephone admitted, shutting her locker. "But if Hades hadn't rushed me home, I would've liked to have stayed and seen more."

Artemis looked at her with admiration. "You're braver than me, then."

"Me too," said Aphrodite. "I wouldn't even know what *outfit* to wear in the Underworld!"

"Maybe something fireproof," Persephone advised.

The other goddessgirls laughed. So what if liking cemeteries and the Underworld made her different from others, Persephone thought. Her friends didn't care. They liked her just the way she was. And it had been fun to wow them with all the sights she'd seen.

She wondered if Pheme got the same thrill whenever she passed on a particularly juicy bit of gossip or an interesting rumor. The difference was, what Persephone had said was *true*.

The herald appeared on the balcony above the girls' heads and struck his lyrebell. "The sixty-sixth day of school is about to begin," he called out.

"See you at lunch," Persephone called to her friends as they split up to go to class. She glanced around as she hurried down the hall, hoping to see Hades. She wanted to apologize for the way she'd acted last night. She wanted to tell him he'd been right to take her home. But he was nowhere in sight.

At the end of third period she joined her friends in the cafeteria for a quick bite. She grabbed a bowl of yogurt topped with pomegranola from the cafeteria and hurriedly spooned it down. Then she stood up. "I've got something I have to do," she told her friends. "I'll see you later." After scurrying out of the cafeteria, she headed for Principal Zeus's office.

When Persephone asked Ms. Hydra if Hades was around, the nine-headed office lady seemed a bit surprised. Still, she knocked on Zeus's door, then opened it a crack. "There's a goddessgirl here to see Hades," said her cheerful, bright yellow head. The other eight remained staring at Persephone.

"Who is she?" Zeus thundered back.

Godness! His voice was so loud and scary Persephone had to fight down the urge to turn and bolt. She reminded herself that Principal Zeus was Athena's *father*, and that Hades had been afraid of Zeus at first too. Now Hades called him "a really great guy."

"What's your name, dear?" asked Ms. Hydra's purple head.

Straightening her spine, Persephone summoned her courage. Since Zeus hadn't told her to go away, Hades must be in there.

"It's me. Persephone!" she shouted through the crack in the door.

9

Principal Zeus's Office

Aftera brief pause, Principal Zeus thrust the door open so hard it ripped loose from its hinges. Looking past him, Persephone caught a glimpse of Hades at a table in the far corner of the room, but then the principal blocked her view.

"Oops!" He grabbed the teetering door before it

could fall on top of her and set it against the outside wall.

"Please ask the custodian to fix that," he told Ms. Hydra.

"Certainly," she replied. "That's the fourth time it's happened this month," her green head whispered to Persephone.

"Well, Persephone, come in!" Zeus boomed.

Nervously she stepped inside the office, sidling past him. She'd seen the principal at a distance in the hallways and on a stage, but she'd never seen him up close before now. It wasn't like he ever hung out with Athena and her friends, after all. He must be nearly seven feet tall, she thought, the way he towered over her. He had bulging muscles and a massive head of wild red hair that was far more unruly than her own red curls.

Remembering her manners, Persephone bravely stuck out her hand. "Thanks for seeing me," she said.

Principal Zeus reached out a meaty paw. A wide, flat golden bracelet encircled his wrist. As he pumped her hand up and down, she felt a tingling sensation as small jolts of electricity passed through her. "Great to see you!" Zeus roared. His piercing blue eyes peered down at her. "I don't know why more students don't visit me. It's almost like they're scared of me or something. Well, come in, come in. Getting along fine in your classes, are you?"

Persephone nodded.

"That's my goddessgirl!" Zeus clapped her on the back, sending her flying across the room while another jolt of electricity zapped all the way down her spine. She landed sprawled halfway across the table where Hades sat, yet somehow managed to stay on her feet.

"Uh, hi," she said, looking at him through her disheveled hair.

"Hi," he said cautiously. His dark eyes searched hers as if to gauge her friendliness—or lack thereof. After the way she'd treated him last night, Persephone couldn't blame him.

As she straightened up, Zeus pointed to the chair next to Hades. "Sit!" he ordered. When she complied, he sat down across the table from them, folding his hands and glancing from one to the other as if waiting for them to speak.

Coming here had seemed like a good idea, but now that she had done it, Persephone felt a little uncertain.

She'd never been inside Zeus's office before, so she studied it with genuine interest to keep from having to explain her visit.

Scattered around were a variety of chairs with big scorch marks on them. An enormous desk littered with papers, file folders, and empty bottles of Zeus Juice took up most of the space. An impressive golden throne sat behind it. It looked like a much more comfortable fit for Zeus than the tiny student chair he was balancing on now.

"Want some of my lunch?" Hades asked, drawing her attention.

"No, thanks," said Persephone, glancing at the two half-eaten plates of nectaroni and cheese.

"Then you won't mind if we finish ours?" asked Zeus.

Scooping up a huge forkful of nectaroni, he shoveled it into his mouth. "Hades here has told me a lot about you," he said, speaking with his mouth full.

"Oh?" Persephone tensed a little and darted a look toward Hades, wondering what he might've said.

Hades straightened, looking somewhat alarmed. Then he cleared his throat, like he was trying to catch Zeus's attention.

Zeus laughed, spewing tiny bits of nectaroni onto the table. "Don't worry. It was all good." He pushed his plate away and patted his stomach. "So," he said, eyeing the two of them.

Across from her, Hades stiffened further, obviously worried about whatever Zeus was going to say.

"Both of you planning to go to the Harvest Hop tomorrow night?"

Huh? Was he hinting that they should go—together? Sometimes grown-ups were *so* unsubtle.

A dark shadow passed over Hades' face as he set down his fork. "I'm busy. Lots of new shades coming in."

Zeus raised an eyebrow. "In the Underworld there are *always* lots of new shades coming in."

"I forgot all about the dance," Persephone admitted. She didn't tell him that, in any case, she hadn't planned to go. She'd thought her mom wouldn't allow it. But last night, of course, things had changed.

"Should be a lot of fun," said Zeus, interrupting her thoughts. "It would be a shame to miss it." He stroked his curly red beard and said slyly, "Maybe you two should go together! Keep each other company, you know?"

She could hardly believe he'd suggested that out

loud! She blushed, and Hades ducked his head. His dusky curls fell forward, hiding his face.

Zeus glanced from him to Persephone and grinned. Rising swiftly, he said, "I—um—need to take care of something. Back in a few." Hades started to stand too. "Stay!" Zeus barked. Then he smiled, gesturing to them. "Lunch period isn't over for twenty more minutes. No reason for you and Persephone to hurry off."

After Principal Zeus left, Hades squirmed in his chair for a moment. "Sorry for rushing you home last night," he said at last. He stared at his plate. "It's not that I didn't want to see you. In fact, I—"

"It's okay," interrupted Persephone. "You were right to send me home."

Hades jerked back in his chair. "I was?"

Persephone nodded. "My mom found out I ran

away. We had a good talk about it. I think she'll let up on me a little more from now on."

"Really?" Hades' dark eyes looked into her pale ones, and he smiled. "That's great."

Persephone's breath caught in her throat. He had the most beautiful eyelashes! And when he smiled, you could really see how cute he was. "Yes," she said. "It *is* great."

A long, uncomfortable pause followed. Hades toyed with his fork, tapping it against the side of his plate. Persephone twirled her hair around one finger, glancing anywhere but at him. Idly she noticed a drooping plant leaning against a file cabinet nearby. It was a poppy, her mom's favorite flower.

"So what do you think of Principal Zeus's idea?" asked Hades.

"What idea was that?" Persephone asked, pretending not to know what he was talking about.

Hades shrugged. "You know. The dance."

"Oh, that," said Persephone. "What about it?"

Hades fell silent for a few moments, brooding. Finally he blurted out, "Will you go with me?"

Persephone smiled. She'd almost given up on him asking! "Thanks. I'd love to." Hades beamed back at her—the widest smile she'd ever seen from him.

They were still smiling as they left the office a few minutes later. Persephone touched Principal Zeus's poppy plant before they went out the door. Instantly its drooping leaves became green and strong, and bright red flowers sprang up all over. "Cool!" said Hades. He reached his hand out to her, and Persephone entwined her fingers with his. Hand in hand they strolled through the open doorway.

At home that evening Persephone told her mom about the dance. "Hades asked me to go with him." She paused. "I said I would."

Demeter stiffened, frowning. "I don't think that's such a good—"

"Come on, Mom, pleeease. It's just a dance," Persephone reminded her. "A *school* dance. Principal Zeus and most of the teachers will be there, so it will be well chaperoned."

"*Zeus* will be there?" Demeter colored slightly, and a soft light came into her eyes.

"Yes," said Persephone. If she didn't know any better,

she'd think her mom had a secret crush! "As a matter of fact, he and Hades are good friends."

"I see." Demeter seemed to be thinking. "Well, if Zeus likes Hades, I suppose he can't be *all* bad."

Persephone hugged her mom. "He's not. Honest."

Demeter sighed. "You're growing up so fast. Someday you'll be leaving home. You won't need me anymore."

"Well I sure need you now," said Persephone, giving her a big smile. "Because I don't know what to wear to the dance!"

Demeter smiled back and put an arm around her. "Let's go look in your closet. And if we can't find anything there, I'll make you the prettiest chiton ever."

As she went to bed that night, Persephone had never felt happier. But just before she fell asleep, a worrisome thought popped into her head. She knew her friends would do their best to welcome Hades, but what about the other godboys and goddessgirls? She was certain they'd all like Hades if they got to know him. But would they give him a chance?

10

The Dance

PERSEPHONE HAD ARRANGED TO MEET HADES at the dance, along with her friends. When he was late, she began to worry that he might not show up. What if he'd changed his mind about coming? Or maybe he got stuck on some errand in Tartarus. The shades there could be awfully whiny and demanding—just like they'd been in life, she supposed.

"Why don't you go in without me?" Persephone said to Aphrodite, Athena, and Artemis as they stood together near the entrance to the gymnasium. "I'm sure Hades will be here soon."

"You won't mind?" asked Aphrodite. She was dazzling in her hot pink chiton. Her gleaming golden hair, threaded with sparkly pink ribbons, hung down her back in loose curls.

"Not at all," said Persephone. They'd already been waiting fifteen minutes. She knew the goddessgirls must be anxious to go inside. And practically every godboy would be waiting to ask Aphrodite to dance. They only had to look at her to fall hopelessly in love with her.

Athena's face lit up. "Look, there's Mr. Cyclops! Maybe I can discuss my Hero-ology project with him."

Persephone grinned. *Trust Athena to be more interested in talking to a teacher about a school project than in the dance itself.*

"Well, if you really don't mind," said Artemis, "Apollo's band will be warming up already." Apollo was Artemis's twin brother. His band, Heavens Above, was playing for the dance.

"Go!" ordered Persephone. She made shooing motions with her hands. As her three friends swept inside, she caught the door before it could close and peered into the gym. It was round and open to the star-filled sky. Flaming torches had been placed at intervals around its perimeter. In the middle, on a raised platform, Apollo plucked at his kithara, a seven-stringed lyre, while Dionysus blew on his double-reeded *aulos.*

Persephone shut the door. Pacing back and forth in front of it, she decided to give Hades ten more minutes to show up. After that she'd just have to swallow her embarrassment at being stood up and go in alone.

"Hi, Persephone!" Pheme called out. Stepping down from a chariot, she approached the gym. Her white linen chiton was cinched at the waist by a thin silver belt, and her spiky orange hair was even spikier than usual. "Waiting for someone?" she asked. Her words puffed into the night air in little cloud letters that quickly faded away.

Persephone eyed her warily. "Maybe."

"Ooh, a godboy, I bet. What's his name?"

Persephone shook her head. "I'm not saying."

"Please," pleaded Pheme. "I won't tell." Lifting her

hand, she twisted her thumb and finger together at the corner of her orange-glossed lips, as if turning a key to lock them shut.

Persephone rolled her eyes. "Right."

Pheme giggled and pushed open the gym door.

A moment later Persephone felt a tap on her shoulder. She spun around. *"Hades!"* she exclaimed, her eyes lighting up. "I was afraid you weren't going to come!" He was wearing a purple tunic that draped around his waist and over one shoulder. The majestic color suited him well. She thought he looked handsomer than ever.

"Aha!" said a voice behind her. Too late, Persephone realized that Pheme hadn't disappeared into the gym after all. She'd been hovering in the open doorway. Now the door banged shut behind her. No doubt she couldn't wait to spread rumors about Persephone and Hades!

"Sorry I'm late," Hades said. "Just as I was leaving, Charon delivered a huge boatload of shades. One of them tried to escape, and Cerberus took after him. Then a fight broke out between the shades of two men who fought as enemies in the Trojan War." He sighed. "It took me a while to help sort things out."

"It's okay," said Persephone, touching his arm. "You're here now."

Hades smiled down at her. "You look beautiful."

Persephone blushed. "Thanks." Feeling self-conscious, she straightened the wreath of daisies atop her red curls. Demeter had made her a gorgeous saffron yellow chiton. Woven through the fabric were sparkling gold and silver threads. But the black velvet cloak she'd thrown over the dress had been her idea.

Aphrodite had rolled her eyes when she saw it. "Interesting fashion statement," she'd said. Persephone didn't care. The combination of light and dark suited her just right.

Hades peered toward the door. "I suppose we have to go in," he said grimly. He didn't sound like he was looking forward to it.

"You're not nervous, are you?" asked Persephone. "My friends will like you. I *promise.* Just be yourself."

Hades frowned.

"Only perhaps not so gloomy," Persephone added. "It is a party, after all."

"I'll try," said Hades. He reached for her hand. The two of them entered the gym, but as they started toward the band, they found their way blocked by a couple of godboys.

Just beyond them stood Pheme. "I'm sorry," she mouthed to Persephone. She certainly hadn't wasted any time! And though she probably hadn't meant any harm, as usual her gossip had stirred up trouble.

Ares stood with his legs apart, his arms crossed in front of his chest. "What are you doing here, Death-boy?" he sneered.

"Yeah," said the beefy-looking godboy next to him. "You don't belong here."

Hades' grip on Persephone's hand tightened.

Ares frowned at his companion. "Let me handle this, Kydoimos." Stepping forward, he poked his finger in Hades' chest. "Why don't you go back to that stink-hole you call home?"

Scowling, Hades knocked Ares' hand away. "Lay off, will you?"

Godness! If ever there was a time to go along to get along, it was now, thought Persephone. Summoning a smile, she looked right at Ares. "We're just here to dance, same as you," she said sweetly. "Aren't we, Hades?" To her surprise her words sounded far calmer than she felt.

After a second, Hades' grip on her hand loosened. "Yeah, that's right," he said, matching her light tone. But his face still looked grim.

By now some of the godboys and goddessgirls nearby had noticed what was happening. They gathered to watch.

Ares swept his eyes over the crowd, then smiled at Hades. "All right. You win." He wheeled around and took two steps away, as if he'd decided to leave Hades alone after all. But in the next second, he whirled toward Hades again. "Or maybe not." He drew back a fist.

Persephone gasped. At that exact moment, Aphrodite pushed through the crowd. Athena and Artemis, accompanied by her dogs, were right at her side. She marched straight up to Ares and dazzled him with a smile. "Want to dance?" she cooed.

Ares' eyes softened. "Um, yeah. Of course I do," he said in a lovestruck voice.

Aphrodite turned toward the dance floor. Seeming to forget all about Hades, Ares unclenched his fist and followed her as if her beauty had cast an enchantment over him.

Suddenly she spun away from him. "Find another

partner, then!" she exclaimed, starting back toward Artemis and Athena. "I don't dance with bullies!"

"What?" Ares sounded confused.

"Get a clue!" Artemis blurted out. "She doesn't *like* bullies."

"Ye gods! Your brain is slower than a horseless chariot!" added Athena.

The crowd burst into laughter.

Ares' face turned purple with rage. His hands balled into fists again, but then, glancing uncertainly at Aphrodite, he unclenched them.

Suddenly, lightning flashed above everyone's head. Zeus's voice boomed out as he strode into the middle of the group. "What's going on?" he demanded. "I can hardly hear myself think with all this commotion."

Persephone couldn't help wondering how he could hear *anything* over his own loud voice.

No one answered Zeus, but he seemed to notice Ares' guilty expression. He glowered at the godboy suspiciously. To Persephone's surprise, Ares practically wilted under his gaze.

Hades glanced back and forth between Zeus and Ares. Finally he seemed to reach a decision, and he spoke up. "Sorry for bothering you, Principal Zeus." He looked at Ares and laughed in a way Persephone could tell he didn't quite mean, but fortunately, Zeus didn't seem to notice. "Next time I ask you to show me your boxing moves, Ares, I guess we should do it outside."

Ares' eyebrows rose, and he shot Hades a surprised, grateful look. "Yeah, I s'pose so, um, buddy."

Bustling over, Aphrodite grabbed Ares' hand and gave him a more genuine smile this time. "That's better. *Now* I'll dance with you."

Ares grinned lopsidedly, looking far more handsome than when he'd been angry. "Okay, Aphrodite, whatever you say." She pulled him toward the dance floor as the crowd broke up.

After they'd gone, Zeus clapped Hades on the back, making sparks fly.

"Ow!" said Hades, barely managing to keep his balance.

Oblivious, Zeus glanced approvingly from him to Persephone. "Glad you two were able to make it. Having fun?"

"Yes, sir," they said at the same time, glancing uncomfortably at each other and then at him. But Zeus didn't seem to take the hint that they felt awkward at the party with him around.

Suddenly Zeus grunted and thumped his forehead in a way that told them he was speaking to Metis, the fly that lived in his head, who was also Athena's mother. "What? I'm not bothering them. Sure, of course I know they don't want grown-ups hanging around when they're trying to have fun, but . . . What? You want to dance? But I'll look like an idiot out there dancing by myself. Oh, okay. Whatever you say, dear." Shaking his head, he went to stand near the edge of the dance floor, where he could discreetly sway to the beat of the music without looking *too* foolish.

Persephone squeezed Hades' hand. "Good job," she said. "What you did with Ares, I mean."

Hades shrugged modestly.

Sometimes going along to get along really was the best choice, thought Persephone. If Hades hadn't defused Ares' anger by pretending they were friends, who knew what could have happened? But there was a time for anger, too. Without it, she might never have cleared the air with her mom and her friends.

Athena and Artemis came up to her and Hades. "Come on, you two," Athena said, giving Persephone's arm a tug. "Let's dance."

Hades held back. "Maybe we should just watch. I'm a really *horrible* dancer."

"You can't be worse than my dad," said Athena, nodding toward Principal Zeus. He seemed to have overcome his initial embarrassment and was now doing a weird sort of mix of the hula, the tango, and the bunny hop.

Persephone winked at Athena and Artemis. Then she grinned up at Hades. "Yeah. Come on, Hades. Everyone knows that the *hottest* new steps come from the Underworld. We're just *dying* to see them." Giggling, the three goddessgirls dragged Hades onto the dance floor.

"It'll be your own fault if I step all over your feet," Hades warned.

Persephone put her hands on his shoulders and smiled up at him. "I'll take the chance."

APHRODITE SLID INTO HER SEAT IN MR.

Cyclops's Hero-ology class just as the lyrebell sounded,

signaling the start of another day at Mount Olympus

Academy. As she tucked her long golden hair, which

was threaded with pink ribbons, behind her delicate

ears, she was aware that every godboy in class was

watching her. Hoping that in her rush to get ready that

morning she hadn't gotten lipstick on her teeth, she lift-

ed her chin and smiled at one of the godboys. Because

he was a centaur, and therefore part horse, he stood at

the back of the room; with four legs it was too difficult to sit in a chair. Dazzled by Aphrodite's attention and sparkling blue eyes, he blushed and glanced away.

A few of the bolder godboys continued to gaze at her, however. Their adoration was plain to see. Ignoring them, Aphrodite reached into her desk and took out her Hero-ology textscroll. As the goddessgirl of love and beauty, she'd grown used to such admiration. Took it for granted, in fact. All her life godboys had found her enchantingly beautiful. It seemed they had only to look at her to fall hopelessly in love. That wasn't her fault, of course. It was just the way things were.

Aphrodite glanced across the aisle at Athena, trying to get her attention. All week in class, the discussions had centered around mortal maidens and youths. She wanted to ask if Athena had heard the intriguing rumors about a maiden on Earth who could run as swiftly as the wind, faster than any youth—or beast even. But as usual, her friend's nose was buried in a textscroll. Before Aphrodite could call out to her, Medusa, who sat directly behind Athena, leaned across the aisle.

Her head writhed with hissing green snakes instead of hair. Their tongues flicked in and out as Medusa poked Aphrodite with one of her long green fingernails. "You were almost late," she sneered. "Troubles, Bubbles?" Medusa and her horrible sisters, Stheno and Euryale, never missed an opportunity to use the awful nickname to make fun of Aphrodite's sea-foam origins.

"Not really," Aphrodite muttered. She wasn't about to admit she'd overslept. It would only give Medusa another reason to poke fun at her. Probably with jokes about her needing lots of beauty sleep. Fortunately, before her snaky green nemesis could say anything more, Mr. Cyclops finished with a student he'd been speaking to and stood up. As his humongous single eye swept the room, everyone fell silent.

Aphrodite wondered what they'd be discussing today. Yesterday their teacher had asked how much and what kind of help they thought gods should give to mortals they favored. Aphrodite, who enjoyed helping mortals in love, had hoped to talk about that, but the godboys in class had immediately steered the discussion toward weapons and war—topics that could never hold her interest for long.

Reaching into her bag, she pulled out her pink papyrus notescroll and began to doodle little hearts all over the front with her favorite red feather pen. Mr. Cyclops cleared his throat. "Today I'd like you to consider the following question," he said. "Need mortal maidens always marry?"

Dropping her red feather pen in surprise, Aphrodite sat up straighter. Now, this was an engaging question! She'd like to see the godboys try to make *this* into a discussion about weapons and war, she thought as she raised her hand high.

"Yes, Aphrodite?" asked Mr. Cyclops.

"I wouldn't want to see any young maiden go unwed," she said. "Everyone should have a chance to fall in love."

"But what if the maiden would rather be alone?" Athena asked. "What if she has other interests, like traveling the world, or becoming a first-class scholar, or . . . or inventing things?"

Aphrodite smiled at her. Poor Athena. She'd never really had a boyfriend. Just wait until she experienced her first crush. She'd think differently then. "If the maiden feels that way, then perhaps it's only because she hasn't yet found the right youth," she said kindly.

"But not all youths marry," Athena pointed out. "So why should all maidens?"

Poseidon thrust his trident into the air. As always, water dripped from it and from him to puddle beneath his chair. "That's because many youths prefer the life of a soldier," he declared.

"That's right!" exclaimed another godboy. "War trumps marriage any day."

Aphrodite rolled her eyes. "Oh, really? And which do you think contributes more to the survival of the human race?"

Mr. Cyclops beamed at her. "Good point."

Just then the school loudspeaker crackled to life. "Attention, godboys and goddessgirls!" thundered Principal Zeus in a deafeningly loud voice. Everyone, including Mr. Cyclops, automatically reached up to cover their ears. "A special assembly on chariot safety starts in ten minutes. Please make your way to the audi-torium."

Looking somewhat annoyed, Mr. Cyclops muttered something about unwarranted interruptions to class time. But then, with a sigh, he said, "All right, everyone. Please line up at the door."

Normally, Aphrodite would have welcomed a chance to get out of class, but not today. Not when the topic of discussion was such an interesting one. Besides, the chariot safety assembly was repeated every year, and it was deadly dull. Who among them didn't know that racing into a turn could cause a chariot to tip over? Duh. Or that you shouldn't ever fly directly into the sun?

After the assembly, which Zeus had livened up with a real demonstration of racing chariots for a change, it was time for lunch. Aphrodite was starved. As she stood in the cafeteria line with Athena and their other two best friends, dark-haired Artemis and pale-skinned Persephone, her stomach began to rumble like a volcano about to erupt.

Her friends laughed. "*Somebody's* hungry," said Artemis.

Aphrodite blushed. "Yes, very." She didn't say it loudly, but considering the response, she might just as well have shouted it. A dozen godboys in line ahead of her whipped around at the sound of her voice, eager to get her attention.

"You can have my spot, Aphrodite!" yelled Poseidon from ten spaces up the line. He took a step toward her, dripping water onto another godboy's sandal-clad feet.

Ares, who was the cutest godboy in school, in Aphrodite's opinion, glowered at him.

"Watch where you're dripping, Fishface!" Droplets of water flew as he shook one foot and then the other. Poseidon glowered back, his mouth opening and closing a couple of times like a fish's.

Ignoring him, Ares turned toward Aphrodite. "Take my place," he said with a charming smile. "I insist."

Aphrodite hesitated. Ares could be a bit of a bully at times, but she had to admit that there was something about him she found . . . well, *irresistible*.

Elite Ambition

Scandals, Rumors, Lies

Ruby's Slippers

Nice and Mean

The Hot List

Odd Girl In

FIVE GIRLS. ONE ACADEMY. AND SOME SERIOUS ATTITUDE.

CANTERWOOD CREST

by Jessica Burkhart

TAKE THE REINS
BOOK 1

CHASING BLUE
BOOK 2

BEHIND THE BIT
BOOK 3

TRIPLE FAULT
BOOK 4

BEST ENEMIES
BOOK 5

LITTLE WHITE LIES
BOOK 6

RIVAL REVENGE
BOOK 7

HOME SWEET DRAMA
BOOK 8

CITY SECRETS
BOOK 9

Don't forget to check out the website for downloadables, quizzes, author vlogs, and more!

www.canterwoodcrest.com

FROM ALADDIN M!X   PUBLISHED BY SIMON & SCHUSTER